CARTOONIA

Scarlett Harrington

Cartoonia series title. Scarlett Harrington Press

Published by: Scarlett Harrington

Copyright © 2020 by Scarlett Harrington

ISBN 978-1-8382951-4-1

TABLE OF CONTENTS

CARTOONIA

PROLOGUE

Rachel opened her eyes and found herself on the cold hard floor of the museum's lobby. Alpha and his pack were gone, together with the objects that had come up at their appearance. All that was left was a dark, cold room with musty relics and antiques. Although she couldn't see well in the dark, she could feel the changes. The air felt heavier and mustier.

She felt her face and body with her hands. Everything was the same, but it wasn't just as perfect as it should be. Rachel was too glad to be free to worry about any changes in her body.

She looked around and found Areeyah not too far from where she stood. At first, she was hesitant about picking it up, but she couldn't leave it lying around on the museum floor. She picked it up and ran her fingers gently around its gold edges. Her friends would have discovered that she was gone by now.

She walked down the hallway towards the museum's entrance door. It was two in the morning, and everywhere was eerily silent. Much to her surprise, she discovered that the door gave way under her gentle push.

With Areeyah clutched to her chest, Rachel walked into the sleepless streets of New York and breathed in the crisp air of the city. She wrinkled her nose in disgust and walked away.

It took her two days to get home. At first, she had roamed the streets, trying to figure out what to do and where to go. But the pieces had fallen into place, and as soon as she remembered her old address, she headed home.

*****

Rebecca sat down at the breakfast table to wait for the others. She hadn't seen Rachel all morning and thought she could be with Ron. Rebecca felt a jab in her heart but decided to keep calm. Jer walked in looking so handsome and irresistible. She remembered the previous night, and she felt wet between her legs. He flashed her a smile and pulled out a chair for himself.

"Rebecca, have you seen Ron and Rachel? I haven't set my eyes on them all morning."

"They're probably together somewhere. Let's eat. They should join us soon."

Rebecca and Jer were almost through with breakfast when Ron walked in. He looked flustered, and Rebecca could sense that something was wrong.

"I thought Rachel was here with you," he said.

Rebecca's heart skipped. She couldn't believe that her worst fears were coming to pass.

Without warning, the ground began to shake. The plates and cutleries rattled violently and fell off the table. There was fear in their eyes as they looked at each other, wondering what was happening.

"Rachel," Rebecca said through gritted teeth.

"What do we do now?" Jer asked. One look at Rebecca gave him the answer he needed.

Rebecca and Ron stood up from their chairs and made to leave when another tremor came on. This time, the ground shook so hard they were afraid the house might split in two and fall on their heads.

Rebecca lost her grip on the table and fell headlong in Jer, who caught her. He wrapped his arms around her and held her close against his body. Jer felt a pleasant jolt through his body as he inhaled the heady scent of her skin. She looked up at him, her eyes filled with terror and a burning need for him.

Jer felt a desire to fill her with his erection, to have his hands running over her smooth, silky skin as she squirmed in ecstasy. Without warning, he covered her lips in his and savored the sweet taste of her lips. Lust fired up in him, and he was oblivious to the chaos around him. All he wanted was the pleasure between

Rebecca's thighs. He laced his fingers through her hair and held her head in place. Rebecca moaned softly and leaned into him; she could feel the length of Jer's desire rubbing against her thighs. The lust for his hard cock consumed her. His hands and the feel of his lips on her nipples and skin. She didn't care that everywhere was breaking down, as long as it crashed with Jer's cock inside her. She wanted to ride to eternity on his cock.

Jer pulled the bow of her halter neck top and freed her breasts, which yearned for his mouth on them. He never ceased to be fascinated by them. For a moment, he forgot the pain and the betrayal. All he wanted was to sate this maddening lust for Rebecca.

Ron had run into his room to pick a few essential things. He had never trusted anything or anyone in Cartoonia. At first, they had all thought that Daffodils was their perfect home in Cartoonia, but now it was about to cave in.

"Hey, guys, I think we should be heading for Anchor before…"

He stopped dead in his tracks when he saw Jer with Rebecca's breast in his mouth. The two were lost in their lust and were unaware of his prescience.

Jer had his head buried between Rebecca's breasts, and she had her hand firmly around his hard cock. She pumped one hand up and down his hard meat while she rubbed her clit with the other hand. Jer was already getting impatient; he couldn't wait to plunge his erection into the soft creamy secrets of her cunt. Jer carried Rebecca to the dining table and pushed the crockery off the table.

Ron jumped at the loud crash, he was so absorbed in watching Jer and Rebecca, and he felt drawn to them.

Jer pushed Rebecca's skirt up her over her waist and spread her legs. She grabbed his hard cock and shoved it into her moistened cunt. Jer thrust and grunted away with such abandon.

Ron couldn't tear his eyes off Rebecca's body. She squeezed her breasts together and moaned as Jer's cock rammed into her. Ron felt his cock nod in his shorts. Suddenly he was overwhelmed with lust for Rebecca, too. He wanted her hands all over him.

Ron was drawn to the pair by Rebecca's moans. He approached them and quickly brought out his cock, which he rubbed against Rebecca's nipple while massaging the other breast with his free hands.

Rebecca writhed in ecstasy, she could feel some power coursing through her body, and she could feel that same power surging through Jer's thrusts and the lust in Ron's eyes. She felt completed by Jer's eagerness to satisfy her craving and Ron's deep affection for her.

Rebecca gently took Ron's hands away from her breasts and put his cock in between her mounds. She rubbed her jugs against Ron's cock as he thrust between the two lovely breasts. The warm, soft feel of Rebecca's boobs on Ron's hard cock, drew out tiny drops of fluids that escaped from his cock. The two men gave and took pleasure from Rebecca's body. Ron and Jer felt distinct yet bound to Rebecca by some bond that tied the three of them.

Rebecca moaned as Jer's breathing increased. He was digging faster and harder, just like Ron was thrusting between her breasts. Waves of ecstasy soared through her, and she cried out as the three of them came at the same time. Ron's fluid splattered all over her breasts, and Jer gave one last thrust and groaned as his liquid spilled inside Rebecca.

"I guess the tremor has stopped," Jer said as he looked around the messy room.

"I think we should leave," Ron suggested.

Jer glanced at Rebecca, who lay on the table in all her naked glory, her face calm and beautiful.

She sat up on the table, and her eyes shone with a new sparkle and enthusiasm.

"It feels good to be home."

CHAPTER ONE

Everyone turned to look at Lily, who began to feel uncomfortable with the sudden attention. She glanced at Peyton whose eyes screamed 'betrayer' at her. She looked at Jamie then at Kyle, who mouthed; *I got you.*

Rebecca noticed the tension among the four. She could already tell who the betrayer would be among them. But she was sure that she would do everything and anything to leave Cartoonia.

"We have to find Areeyah," Rebecca said.

They continued their meal in silence. Lily noticed that Ron couldn't stop staring at Peyton's breasts. She smiled quietly as an idea crossed her mind. Kyle caught her smiling, and she blinked her lashes at him and blew him a kiss. Ron chose that moment of distraction to smile lustfully at Peyton, and she blushed.

"As you already know, your survival in Cartoonia depends on a lot of things. Cartoonia will offer you the perfection and luxury you have always fantasized about but at a price. You must do what it requires of you as often as possible. Understanding this rule is very important if you don't want to starve or get lost before you can make your way out of here," Rebecca explained.

"Like always and whenever Cartoonia demands?" Peyton asked.

"Yes, whenever Cartoonia demands and with whom it wants. Cartoonia has made its choice, but along the way, things happen, and decks get shuffled. You still have to go along with the tide if you want to stay afloat."

They continued the rest of their meal in silence as they pondered over what Rebecca had said.

After the meal, they all helped to clear the table. Peyton retreated into her room to check out her new clothes and explore other content in her room.

Lily was taking a walk along the beach when she heard someone call her name.

"Hey Lily, wait up," Jamie called out to her.

She turned around, and desire stirred somewhere in her belly when she saw him coming towards her in a sleeveless beach top and pants that hugged his athletic form. The wind blew his short curly hair off his face giving him an irresistible appearance.

"What are you doing here?" Jamie asked as soon as he caught up with her.

"I was just curious and came to see if Anchor is still here; turns out she returned all by herself," Lily replied.

Jamie put his hand over his brows and scanned the horizon; the ship was nowhere to be found. It seemed they would never leave Cartoonia.

His heart sank, and he looked at Lily. She didn't seem sad or worried about the situation. Jamie wished he could share her optimism.

The sun began to set in the west, and they stood together watching the spectacular colors the twilight cast across the sky. The yellow and red hues were more vivid than they remembered and the dash of green across the clouds made everything look so perfect. Jamie looked at Lily, the short sundress cinched at her waist, making it more pronounced, and curvy. Her nipples were barely concealed by the flower print on the dress, leaving her breasts in the full glare of his view. Jamie noted how the glowing sky lit up her face and hair, and he fought hard against the strong urge to make love to her right there on the beach.

Lily turned around and looked into Jamie's handsome face. He touched her brown hair and felt the silky softness between his fingers. She felt a strong urge to trace her finger across his cheek and kiss his lips. She was still fantasizing when she felt moist lips over hers. She was dazed by the suddenness and the heady taste of Jamie's lips on hers; it felt so wrong yet so thrilling. She allowed herself to get intoxicated by her overwhelming need for him. Her knees buckled beneath her, and she became oblivious to everything around her. What she felt for Jamie was more than just an obsession over his good looks. She moaned as his hands slipped behind her back, deftly tracing lines of hot desire along her spine. Lily moaned into his mouth, her hands seeking the rising bulge that was constrained by his pants.

The wind carried the sound of laughter to them, and they broke their kiss. Jamie and Lily saw Peyton and Kyle walked towards them from the meadow.

"I don't think they saw us, did they?" Jamie asked anxiously.

"No, they didn't, and they couldn't even if they tried," Lily replied.

She walked off to meet Kyle, leaving Jamie to wonder just how much she knew and how much power she wielded.

CHAPTER TWO

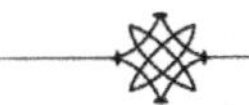

Peyton woke up to the smell of fried bacon and freshly baked pie. She was hungry and exhausted after the rough sex with Jamie the previous night. He had fucked her like a starving beast unleashed from its prison. She opened her door and walked into the hallway to get to the kitchen. She noticed one of the double doors was slightly open. She was curious and drew closer to the door; she listened carefully for any sound before she peeped through the keyhole. There was a library of books and figurines that adorned the shelf.

Peyton looked around to see if anyone was coming down the hallway before she pushed the door and walked into the room. She wasn't prepared for the surprise that met her.

Right there in the middle of the room was a giant golden globe covered in a swirling mist of dazzling colors. Peyton had never seen anything so beautiful and enchanting; she felt drawn to the globe and stepped closer. The colors danced in her eyes, and she felt the mist on her face. She closed her eye, letting its calm wash over her. She wondered what it would feel like to touch the globe. She reached out to touch it, and she heard a voice behind her.

Peyton turned on her heels and found no one else in the room. She heard the voice again, followed by a moan. She noticed that there was another door behind her that led out of the room. It had a magnificent archway and a golden knob. Just like the first door, it was slightly open, and she could hear moans and grunts coming from the room.

"Give it to me, Becky; you know I can't get enough of you."

Peyton drew closer and gasped when she saw Ron thrusting away in Rebecca's mouth. She watched as he pulled out his big cock and shoved it back into Rebecca's mouth. Peyton couldn't see the full length of his cock because it was buried deep in her mouth. Yet, she felt her nipple hardening against her nightshirt as she watched Ron circularly moving his hips as his cock filled Rebecca's mouth.

Peyton's eyes widened when Ron pulled out his hard cock from Rebecca's mouth. It was the biggest cock she had seen, and she felt a tinge of jealousy that Rebecca had it all to herself. Ron spread Rebecca's legs and buried himself inside her, and she arched her back to give him more depth, and her cries filled the room. Peyton could feel her cunt dripping wet with her juice as Ron fucked Rebecca.

She was intrigued by Ron's cock and lost track of time. A moan escaped from her lips, and Ron looked up at the door. Their eyes locked briefly, and Peyton hurried away from the room. Thankfully, Rebecca was deeply wrapped in ecstasy to realize what just happened.

Peyton rushed back to her room and closed the door behind her. Her heart beat wildly, and for a moment, she thought Ron and Rebecca might come after her. Peyton feared they might punish her, not for walking in on their sexcapade but for intruding into what was Rebecca's secret chamber. She slid down the door and wondered if she should tell Jamie or keep everything to herself. She decided to try out another idea.

Peyton took her time soaking herself in the rose bubble bath. Kyle had picked the rose petals the previous day. He had brought more than Lily wanted and had to give some to Peyton. When she stepped out of the bath, she was enveloped in a refreshing scent of wild rose.

She went to her closet and picked out a crop top with a plunging neckline that showed off her big boobs and the flawless skin on her midriff. She paired it with a pair of silver heels and a very short skirt that left very little to the imagination.

The others were already seated at the table when she arrived. She beamed a smile and murmured an apology before taking a seat beside Jamie. She looked around the table and blushed when her eyes met Ron's.

"Now that we are all here," Rebecca said as she cut the pie into slices and took hers, "I guess I have to inform you all that there are simple tasks that we have to carry out daily. Jer will tag the boys along while I work with the girls."

Kyle trudged along quietly behind Jamie as they walked to the meadow. Jamie was his best friend and roommate, but he felt resentment towards him, especially with Lily's growing interest in Jamie. The thought of Jamie making love to Lily filled him with wild rage, but he padded to the orchard where Jer was waiting for them.

*****

Peyton was out in the meadow walking through the field of sunflowers. Rebecca had suggested that Lily and Peyton should spend some time with her and get to try out some recipes for dinner. Lily had followed Rebecca's instruction correctly and had even liked her eggs beaten the way Rebecca liked it. She was lousy at such stuff, and she knew it and never bothered about it. Back home in New York, her dad had a chef who prepared all their meals, and while in college, she had always gone out for her meals or ordered dinner.

She couldn't stay until the end, so she quietly slipped away into the meadow to have some peace.

As she lay there watching the clouds floating across the sky, she heard someone approaching. She looked up and saw Ron. He smiled at her before dropping down by her side.

"Hey, what are you doing out here all by yourself?" Ron asked her with his eyes fixed on her big breasts.

"I needed to catch my breath while Lily and Rachael talked endlessly about magical recipes that could cook fluffy flying cakes for unicorns."

Ron threw back his head and laughed. Peyton smiled at him. He looked down at her breasts again, and Peyton almost froze when Ron's hand reached out and touched her breasts.

"It's just a petal," Ron said, showing her a yellow petal in his hand.

His touch lingered on her skin, and she couldn't deny that she wanted his hands all over her body. Peyton wanted him to fill her cunt with his cock, and she wanted to know what it would feel like to have a dick as massive as Ron's inside her.

Without any warning, Ron grabbed her and kissed her lustily; his warm breath on her cheeks fueled the passion burning inside her. She didn't care if Cartoonia wanted this or not. All that mattered was sating the deep craving she had for Ron's dick.

Ron was glad that Peyton didn't resist. From the day he had seen her on Daffodil, he had thought of nothing but getting his hands on those breasts and fucking Peyton. Ron hadn't forgotten the consequences of what happened between Rebecca, Rachel, Jer, and him. But Ron was confident that he wouldn't be betraying anyone by having sex with Peyton. Just this once, he had told himself.

Ron felt excited when his hands wrapped around the soft, warm skin of Peyton's breasts. They were firm and beautiful, just as he had imagined. Ron sucked hungrily at one nipple and slid his finger under her skirt. He got harder on discovering that she wore nothing else under her miniskirt. Peyton was just as naughty as Ron had imagined and only as yielding. He quickly unbuckled his belt and popped out his long hard cock. Peyton held it in her hands with a smile. Finally, she had the biggest cock in her hands, and she was about to fill her moist cunt with it.

"Fuck me, Ron, "she said, looking into Ron's handsome face as she circled her clit with his dick head. Ron plunged into her, and she cried out at the sheer pain of Ron's cock stretching her tight cunt. Ron pulled back for a second and then pushed his dick slowly inside Peyton. This time, her cunt yielded to his intrusion, and she moaned loudly as he thrust hard and fast.

Peyton wrapped her legs around Ron and screamed his name as he rammed into her. For a moment, she thought she heard a rustling among the flowers. The rhythm of Ron's big dick inside her was driving her insane, and she didn't care if a dragon tore down the meadow, breathing fire through its nostrils.

Ron grabbed her butt and lifted her hips so he could plunge deeper into her and spill his cum. Peyton writhed in ecstasy, wishing he would never stop. She wrapped her hands around his neck and pulled him closer to her breasts. Ron nibbled at her nipples, driving Peyton over the edge. Peyton's climax was quickly followed by Ron's ejaculation and let her hold him in an embrace as he caught his breath.

They heard footsteps approaching, and Ron hurriedly drew up his shorts and sneaked away.

Peyton stood up, pulled her skirt into place, and lay in the grass with her eyes closed, pretending to fall asleep.

"Hey, Peyton."

Kyle carried a small basket of fruits and flowers and was surprised to see Peyton sleeping in the meadow. He watched her closely, noticing how flushed she looked. Peyton opened her eyes and smiled at him.

"Kyle, what are you doing here?" she yawned tiredly.

"I heard some weird noises and decided to come and see what's happening," he said.

"Thanks, Kyle. I just needed some time to myself."

"It's getting dark, and I think we should head back to the Daffodil Manor," Kyle suggested.

Rebecca was incensed when Kyle and Peyton got to the Manor.

"You scheming, selfish bitch," Rebecca spat at Peyton, her eyes flashing with anger. "You never bothered to think of the consequences of your stupid actions before giving in to the whims of your lusty cunt."

Peyton was shocked. Had Ron confessed to Rebecca? Did Cartoonia have that effect on them? She looked at Jamie's face; he was deeply hurt and felt so sorry that she was the one to cause him so much pain. Kyle looked at her without saying anything and simply walked to Lily's side.

"Ron, you should know better than this, "Rebecca shot at Ron, who was also in the room.

"And you, Lily, if you hadn't come here with your pack of friends, we wouldn't be facing this trouble."

"Rebecca, Areeyah brought us here. We didn't choose to be here in the first place." Lily intoned.

"Speaking of Areeyah, where have you hidden it?"

"I've told you before that we don't have it." Lily held Rebecca's gaze until she stormed away.

"Oh Jamie," Peyton went over to Jamie, but he turned his back on her and walked away. She ran after him, but Jamie went into his room and shut the door in her face. Peyton's heart broke into a thousand pieces as she sat at Jamie's door and wept her eyes out.

Kyle and Lily were the only ones left behind. Kyle knew that Peyton's betrayal would create a window for Jamie to seek solace in Lily's arms. He had to act fast to establish his territory.

"Lily, you are the firestorm now; where do we go from here, what do we do?" Kyle inquired.

"Nothing's happening, for now. Rebecca is just mad that Peyton stole her favorite, but Jamie's hurt," Lily explained.

Kyle put his arm around her waist and walked her to his room. As soon as they were inside, he held her face in his hands and gazed adoringly into her eyes. Kyle could feel his soul calling out to hers. He brushed his lips against hers, and she chuckled softly. Kyle thought he saw some spark in her eyes, and his heart warmed up to her. Slowly he deepened his kiss and held her close against him. Lily could feel the length of his hard cock rubbing against her belly, and she moaned softly. Her moaning seemed to urge Kyle. He slipped his hand underneath her top and covered one peach breast with his hand. Kyle squeezed her breast gently, and she moaned his name.

"Kyle, now, please."

Kyle didn't wait for a second request before turning Lily around and made her touch her toes. He pulled down her pants and plugged his throbbing dick into her wet pussy. Lily felt a connection with Kyle as he plunged in and out of her wet cunt. She felt like she was floating on clouds, and she didn't want to come down.

She noticed a light coming from Kyle's closet, but she didn't stop what she was doing with Kyle. She couldn't let go of Kyle's dick at that moment.

Kyle grabbed her hips and thrust harder. Lily noticed that the harder he hit her cunt, the brighter the light in his closet shone. She got down on all fours, jutting her hips out at Kyle, who pushed his hard cock deeper into her. By now, the closet door was shining, and it got brighter as they climaxed.

"What is that? " Lily asked Kyle as soon as he had recovered his breath.

Kyle looked away, pretending not to hear her question.

"Wait a minute, Kyle. You stole the key to Areeyah, and you hid it in your closet?"

"The key to Areeyah?" Kyle was stunned.

"Yes, there's a globe somewhere in the Manor, and that key would open it and reveal a lot of things we need to know."

Without asking, Lily went to Kyle's closet and opened the door. There on the floor of his wardrobe was a silver amulet shaped like a huge dildo. Lily picked it up and felt power surge through her. She closed her eyes as the magic washed over her. Suddenly an irresistible urge to have the dido inside her took over Lily. She looked at Kyle with fiery lust, and he stepped back a little. He had never seen her so powerful yet so horny at the same time.

Kyle looked on in amazement as she put the dildo in her mouth and licked it like an enormous lollipop. She pulled it in and out of her mouth, covering it with saliva and licking it up again. Kyle watched as Lily rubbed the dildo on her breasts. He felt somewhat jealous that Lily was obsessed with the dildo and didn't give a hoot about his cock. He felt angry and ignored. She moaned when she ran the dildo over her midriff down to her hairy cunt. Lily spread her legs wide and circled the dildo around her clit. She shook it vigorously against her wet cunt and moaned words that Kyle couldn't comprehend. Lily squirmed in ecstasy as the dildo pumped itself in and out of her filling her with its size.

There was a loud creak, like the sound of a huge door scraping across the floor, as Lily squirted. Kyle looked around but couldn't see anything. Then he looked at Lily. She lay motionless on the floor, her legs wide open with the hot juice of her cunt still dripping onto the floor. Strangely, the dildo was nowhere to be found; it seemed to have vanished into thin air. Lily started glowing from within; she was covered in the same light coming from the amulet when it was inside Kyle's closet. He was too scared to shout or touch her.

Kyle backed away and headed for the door. It was jammed, he shook the knob vigorously, and it wouldn't budge. He banged his fist against the door in frustration. Kyle closed his eyes in dejection and sank to the floor. He suddenly felt someone touch his hair; he looked up and saw Lily smiling at him.

CARTOONIA
*****

Rebecca woke up when she heard the sound. She turned around, and Jer put his big arm across her breast and squeezed it. Rebecca gently pulled his arm away and stood up from the bed. She grabbed her satin dressing robe and fastened it securely around her body before stepping out of her room. Rebecca glanced at Ron, who lay on the sofa at the other end of the room. She was moved by the calm, peaceful look on his face and was tempted to touch his face, but she steeled herself against doing so. He had betrayed her, and she would not forgive him so easily. It would have been different with Jer, though.

She walked into her ante-room and gasped when she saw the bright light glowing from the middle of the room. The swirling mist had lifted, and in its place was the glowing light. The figurines on the table looked like real miniature people. They no longer had the tarnished look they wore when Rebecca picked them from the beach.

From the first day they had arrived at Daffodil, Rebecca had been in the habit of taking a walk along the beach at sunrise to pick figurines that washed up the shore. Sometimes there was nothing for weeks. A couple of figurines had disappeared when Rachel left Cartoonia; Rebecca believed she must have taken it along with her.

The light grew brighter, and Rebecca ran back into the room to wake Jer and Ron.

"Hey guys, wake up. Something's happening," Rebecca shook Jer.

Jer's eyes flung open, and he stared at Rebecca, confused. Rebecca pointed to the other room, and Jer sprang up from the bed. By now, the light was so bright it almost blinded his eyes.

"What in the world of Cartoonia is going on here, Bec?" Jer asked as he closed the door.

"I have no idea. Do you think it has to do with something Ron and Peyton did?" Rebecca asked.

"I fear so," Jer replied.

Jer rushed to the other end of the room and dragged Ron out of the sofa. He slapped him across the face to wake him up.

"Hey, you, see what you've done? You betrayed us before, and now you are doing it again."

Jer slapped him again across the face, this time, Ron tried to ward off the blow, but it was too late. Rebecca watched on in silence; Ron didn't deserve any pity for what he did to her.

The two men rolled over the floor, but Jer was too much of a match for Ron. He picked him up and flung him across the bed. Ron quickly got and scampered away to the door. He opened it quickly and ran out only to bump into Jamie; both of them crashed to the ground.

CHAPTER THREE

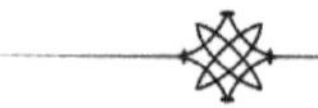

Peyton rushed to Jamie to make sure he was okay. She tried to touch him, but he pushed himself away from her.

"Jamie, are you okay?" Lily asked him.

"Yes, what's going on here?" Jamie asked, rubbing his head.

"Do you realize that you guys are intruding on my privacy?" Rebecca threw back.

Lily had noticed the figurines around the room; there was something unique about each of them. She had known she could not trust Rebecca or anyone else. Lily had doubted Rebecca when she had said she had told them all they needed to know about Cartoonia.

"I'm sorry, Rebecca, Areeyah led us to the place," she apologized.

"I don't care, this is still my chambers, and I don't like people walking in like they own the place."

Lily studied Rebecca carefully. Beneath Rebecca's supposed annoyance at their intrusion, she could sense that she was trying to hide something.

"What are these?" Kyle reached out his hand to pick one of the figurines off the shelf.

"No, don't touch that stuff," Lily yelled.

Kyle's hands froze in mid-air, but his eyes were fixed on the object. He moved towards the item.

"No, Kyle. Stop, don't do it." Lily cried out.

Kyle didn't seem to hear Lily at all. He kept moving and was about to pick up the figurine when Ron rushed towards him and pushed him away from the shelf. Kyle struggled to free himself, but Ron pinned him to the floor.

Lily rushed to Kyle's side and held his face to hers.

"Look at me, Kyle, listen to me, and no matter what happens, don't touch those stuff. Now get up. "

"Any idea what those things are?' Jamie asked Lily.

She looked at Rebecca, who shrugged indifferently. She picked them up because she had made a hobby of collecting them.

"Those are figures of people who have been in Cartoonia and people they know in the real world outside Cartoonia." Lily began to explain. "The other irregularly shaped objects are series of events that have taken place over the years. It's some sort of data collection. When someone leaves Cartoonia, their figurines disappear; hence their information is wiped off from Cartoonia's database."

The others looked on in bewilderment.

"Everybody stand around the table and hold hands," Lily instructed.

They all formed a circle around the glowing globe. There was a blinding flash followed by a loud noise like the same sound that had woken Rebecca. There was silence for a moment, then an image formed on the globe. Rebecca gasped when she saw Rachel's image.

Rachel got home and met her parents, who had been searching for Rachel and her sister over a year ago. They had given up hopes of finding her alive. They were overjoyed at seeing Rachel, but their joy turned a little sour when they found out that Rebecca didn't come home with her. To everyone else, Rachel seemed to have no memory of anything that had happened after that day at the museum. She thought no one would believe her if she told them about Cartoonia.

They would think she had some issues and send her off to therapy. The last thing Rachel wanted was spending hours at the shrink's trying to blame someone for her terrible yet magical experiences.

A mist swirled inside the globe, and when it cleared, Lily and the others could see Rachel thrashing about in bed. She was having a nightmare and woke up with a start. Next, there was an image of Rachel crying over Rebecca's photo.

A sob caught in Rebecca's throat, but she remained calm.

A middle-aged man walked into the room and put his arms around Rachel; he said something to her.

"I know you miss your sister. Your mom and I also do, but we can only hope that someday she turns up just the way you did, "he said.

"It's so sad that you have no memory of what happened back there. It would have given the police some clue."

Rebecca wiped off a tear with her arm. She could only imagine the pains her parents had to go through since she went missing.

Next, they saw Rachel walking down a rather lonely street at night. She walked into one of the houses on the road and quickly climbed the stairs. Rachel knocked at a small door, and a little old man with long beards that almost touched his pockets opened the door.

Rachel quickly introduced herself, and the older man ushered her into his room,

"I want to know how Areeyah can take me back to Cartoonia," Rachel told the man.

"You can't go back to Areeyah, Rachel. You know the rules," the old man replied.

"We know you betrayed the rest and paid a huge sacrifice so you could come back to the real world and figure out how to bring back the rest. You were the only one who did everything required of you, and right now, those things haunt you. But the others will always think you betrayed them. They will never forgive you for leaving."

"Then, how do I rescue my sister?" Rachel wailed.

"There is no way for now. Even if you go in there, would you sacrifice yourself for her?"

Rachel thought about it carefully, and there was so much sadness in her eyes.

"I regret hurting them, especially Rebecca. Someday I will find my way back and bring her home. " Rachel said.

After a brief pause, Rachel picked up the book and walked to the door.

"I have to go now," she whispered, clutching Areeyah close to her chest.

"Be careful with that book, Rachel. I'll advise you to put it away somewhere safe until we can figure out how to rescue your sister."

Rebecca couldn't hold back the tears when she realized that Rachel had sacrificed a lot in trying to rescue her.

They saw Rachel putting the book away in a box in an attic, probably in their house. She locked the box securely and put the key in a locket, which she wore around her neck.

They later saw Rachael walking along a park with a little girl who held her hand tightly as she pointed out some birds and people.

"Mom, can you see that big black birdie over there?" the little girl asked.

"Yes, sweetheart," Rachel replied.

"Mom, can I have your locket? It's gorgeous, and I'd love to wear it."

Rachel smiled at the little girl and put the locket on her neck, and then she hugged her as tightly as she could.

The mist swirled again inside the globe, the colors swirled around violently, and for a moment, they thought the globe would break into pieces.

When the mist cleared, there was an image of a girl with Rachel's locket around her neck. She knelt before the box, which looked like the same box Rachel had put Areeyah in, but this time the colors were brighter and stunning. She ran her hands slowly over its lid.

She pulled the chain over her head and opened the box with the key she found in the locket. She carefully pulled out Areeyah from the box. She scrutinized it, running her hands around the edges of the book. She shut the lid of the box and clutched Areeyah to her chest as she walked away.

It was Lily who found Areeyah again.

CHAPTER FOUR

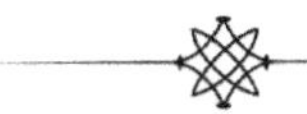

The globe went dark; instead of bright colors, smoke swirled around it. It looked ominous, and everyone waited with bated breath.

Everybody was surprised to learn that Lily was Rachel's daughter. Rebecca wasn't too happy about this. Although she just found out that Rachel had left Cartoonia to find a way to get all of them out, she still resented her for having a normal life. Rebecca had always wished to meet the love of her life, have kids, and raise a large family. She had also missed her parents sorely, and of course their brother too. He had married and moved away to Scotland when the girls were still in college.

Tim and Rebecca had gotten along quite well before he joined the army. He had dotted on Rebecca and Rachel so affectionately, and they had shared beautiful memories.

"Jamie, Jamie," a tiny voice echoed from the globe.

Jaime drew closer, and he could see his mom happily running to the door. Someone had called at the house, and his mother thought it was Jamie.

She opened the door, and when she saw it wasn't Jamie, the smile vanished from her face.

He watched her break down in tears and crumple into a piteous heap before his dad came down the hallway to pick her. Jamie's dad apologized to the guest before taking her away.

Jamie could see two policemen searching the room he had shared with Kyle at the dorm. The police had turned everything inside out to search for clues that could help the police trace their disappearance.

Jamie's eyes misted when he saw his mom huddled on his bed, crying her eyes out. Peyton squeezed his hand gently and whispered reassuring words in his ears. He had felt like yelling at Lily, but he realized that they were also people who had been worry sick about her.

Peyton didn't look the least bothered for all she cared. She was glad she was permitted to have sex with one man she had always crushed on. She could see her dad through the globe, shouting nearly impossible orders at his men. She was glad to be far away from him, where she could make her own decisions without having him breathing down her neck all the time.

Lily broke away from the group, and everything went back to normal. The mist of bright colors swirled around the globe, and the figurines looked tarnished again.

"What do we do now, Lily?" Jamie asked.

"We find Areeyah. Tomorrow morning, Anchor will be at the beach, and we would go to the Ibex island by sunrise," Lily answered.

Everyone began to leave the room, and Rebecca called Lily back.

"I would like to talk to you for a few minutes," Rebecca said.

"Go ahead."

"Where's your mom?" Rebecca asked.

"She's dead."

Rebecca's beautiful face contorted with pain.

"I'm sorry about that," she sympathized.

"It's okay."

"And your dad?"

"I never met my dad, and my mom never spoke about him. We were relatively happy living with my grandparents, and when they died, my mom inherited the house. I had an uncle I saw mostly during the holidays."

Rebecca studied Lily carefully, and then she shook her head in dismay.

"Is something wrong?" Lily asked.

"No, not really."

Rebecca was faced with the possibility that Lily could be either Jer's or Ron's child. Rachel had not only betrayed her but had a child for the only man she had ever loved. She couldn't stand Lily's sight anymore.

"Lily," she said in a menacing tone, "get the hell out of my room, now."

Lily was stunned but left the room without asking any questions.

****

Jer gently flicked away Rebecca's shiny hair from her breast. He slowly traced the outline of her soft mounds with his finger and watched her beautiful face as he rubbed his thumb on her exposed nipple. She murmured something in her sleep and turned on her side, facing away from him. Her big ass was pushed up against his thigh, making his cock grow hard with desire for her cunt. He wanted to grab her butt and thrust his hard cock into her cunt while she slept, but he had other plans for tonight. Jer grabbed Rebecca's ass and gave it a slight jiggle, but she was deeply asleep and didn't move a muscle in response.

Jer heard Ron sleeping soundly on the couch. He couldn't share the bed with them because Rebecca had not forgiven him for his indiscretion with Peyton. From the look of things, Ron would spend many more nights on that couch.

Rebecca had had sex with Jer that night, and they had tortured Ron by making him watch them as they licked up and ravished each other. At some point, Ron couldn't take it anymore and wanted to leave the room only to find the door locked. He had no choice but to go into the bathroom and wait it out. Jer had felt some remorse for poor Ron, but he was more than happy to have Rebecca all to himself.

He crept out of bed and walked to the door. He gently opened it to avoid waking up the other two. He sneaked into the anteroom, taking care to shut the door behind him carefully.

Jer walked across the room to the shelf where Rebecca kept the figurines. They looked so lifeless and dumb in the pale light.

Jer looked at each one carefully, trying to figure out if there was anything familiar about them. He was also curious to know what had happened to his family.

There were so many rows on the shelf, and he didn't know where to start looking.

An idea occurred to him. If the upper shelves contained the oldest figurines, he could find the lower shelves' recent ones.

It took him a while, but he found what he was looking for at the bottom shelf. There they were; four figurines explicitly made the way they were when the four of them had arrived at Daffodils.

He shoved them into the pocket of his sweat pants and went back to the room.

Rebecca felt her hand around the bed and discovered Jer wasn't there. She thought he had gone to the bathroom but couldn't find him there.

Since Rachel left, the three of them had always slept together on the same bed except for Ron's misbehavior. They had sated her appetite with their hard cocks every morning before she went to the beach. Now she had sent Ron to the Coventry, and she couldn't take the chance of having Jer do anything silly. The minutes went by, and there was no sign of Jer. She heard a sound coming from the anteroom and quickly rushed to see what it was.

Jer turned the doorknob, and it swung open. He came face to face with Rebecca. He thought she was sleeping and wouldn't notice he was gone.

"Rebecca," he chuckled nervously, " I thought I heard some noise and had to check it out."

"Oh, and I tried waking you, but you were too far gone."

Rebecca looked him over and went back to bed. Her slim waist emphasized her big ass. She walked gracefully, and her ass jiggled as she moved. Jer was mesmerized, and he almost confessed his sin to her. He shook his head to clear the thoughts. But his cock had a mind of its own, and it pointed towards Rebecca. He took off his sweatpants and carefully folded them before grabbing Rebecca from behind. She giggled as Jer bent her over the bed and began to pump her impatiently.

CHAPTER FIVE

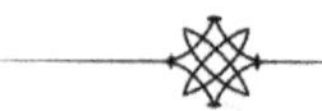

"Where's Peyton?" Jaime asked Kyle as they walked to the beach.

"Probably getting ready for the voyage," Kyle replied. "Perhaps you should go and check on her."

Jamie gave Kyle a withering glare. Lily was already on board Anchor when they got to the shore. She waved excitedly at Kyle and Jamie as they approached the pier.

"Come on board, gentlemen," Lily called out excitedly.

Kylie and Jamie climbed the gangway and got onboard Anchor. Jamie couldn't take his eyes off Lily. She wore a bandeau bikini and paired it with a caramel denim high waist short that showed off some of her butt cheeks. The sun was in her face and the wind in her hair as she smiled at Jamie. He grew hard instantly and had to turn away quickly to avoid the embarrassment.

Kyle put his arm around Lily and kissed her on the lips. He grabbed the butt cheek peeping out of her shorts and gave it a slight squeeze. He traced his lips down her neck, and Lily moaned softly. Kyle grabbed the other butt cheek and kneaded it. He looked over Lily's head and shot Jamie a warning look. Jamie called his bluff and walked away.

Kylie gave Lily one more kiss before letting her go.

"Lily, let's go and check the supplies. I hope we have enough to last us a century, or does Cartoonia say it could be more?"

Lily giggled, "We'll get to Ibex, pick up the amulet and head back to Daffodil today.

The trio watched as Peyton and Rebecca approached the ship.

Rebecca carried a basket of fruits, and Ron and Jer followed closely behind them with more blankets and some wood.

"Hey Peyton, get on here quickly. We don't have much time," Kyle yelled at Peyton as she stood on the shore, wondering how she would get on board without climbing the gangway.

"I wish Cartoonia could give us superpowers just when you need it," she whined.

Jer picked her up and carried her up the gangway into the ship.

"There you got your superpower," Rebecca called out.

They all laughed.

Lily checked the lines while Jamie pulled the lines out of their cleats and off the winches. Kyle and Peyton went under the deck to get breakfast ready. Lily hoisted the sail and headed west in the direction of Ibex. The ship ran along, splashing merrily through the waves. The sea was calm, and the weather promised more sunshine.

Peyton sat on a crate and watched Kyle fix breakfast. She was amazed at how he managed to arrange the breakfast tray perfectly with the ship bouncing up and down like a balloon.

"I think you should apologize to Jamie. He can't stay mad at you for long," Kyle suggested to Peyton.

Peyton remained quiet. She had never felt so guilty and helpless at the same time. Kyle was right, but how could she get Jamie to listen to her. Deep down, she still wanted to be with Ron. She had lied to herself that she only wanted a taste of his big hard cock, but she hadn't stopped thinking about him since that day in the meadow.

"I'll try again, but if he refuses to listen this time, I think I'll have to wait it out," Kyle replied.

Finally, breakfast was ready, and Peyton helped Kyle carry the trays to the deck. She stopped in her tracks when she heard Jamie laughing so heartily at something Lily had said. Her jealousy got the better of her, and she stomped towards Lily.

"Being Cartoonia's favorite pet doesn't give you the right to bitch around my man. Stay away, Peyton yelled at Lily.

Lily was stunned, but she quickly regained her composure and gave attention to the sails.

They were silent for the rest of the voyage except for Lily giving out instructions and reminding the others about being careful on Ibex. It was a treacherous island, and you never knew what surprises it might spring up.

By mid-morning, they arrived at a mountainous island covered in flowers of different colors imaginable. The beautiful flora gave off a heady perfume that could be smelled from many miles away. It looked so enchanting and peaceful.

The crew gazed in wonder as they disembarked the ship and walked up the rocky shores that lead to the beach.

"Don't be fooled by its beauty. Our task is to find the amulet and take it safely back to Daffodil. This island will test your patience, and it will test your strength as well as our friendship with each other. No matter how tough it gets, keep loving, stay optimistic and please only profess love. If you didn't do all these, silence would suffice. Now let's get going. We've got a long way to go."

Peyton was barely listening to Lily, and she was preoccupied with thoughts about winning Jamie back. She followed the rest as they got to the foot of a mountain with its sides looking like pineapple skin. She looked up to the peak and decided that there was no way she was going up that gigantic piece of rock.

Lily and the boys were already up when they noticed Peyton wasn't climbing with them.

"Hey Peyton, need some help?" Kylie called out.

Peyton shook her head, "There's no way I'm climbing up that thing," she protested.

"Peyton, you have to; that is the rule," Lily said.

"How sure are you that you understand what the rule is? As I said, there's no way I'm going up there."

Lily turned around and continued climbing with the others. They were halfway up the mountain when they saw Peyton making her way up. They smiled at each other and waited for her to meet them. When they got to the top, they found a very lush orchid with butterflies flitting around. The place was breathtakingly beautiful. They could see the turquoise sea rolling away into the horizon.

"This is so beautiful," Lily nodded in agreement.

Ibex was beautiful but dangerous, they were running out of time, and she could feel it. They spent the next hour searching for the amulet. It was set in stone and hidden in the orchid. They found out that the amulet was only guarding the main object they were looking for. Set in the middle of the amulet was the most beautiful diamond they had ever seen. It shone so brightly even in the thick undergrowth.

Jamie reached out to pick it, but Lily stopped him.

"The only way to pick it out of that stone is to give Cartoonia what it wants."

Kyle gave Lily a knowing smile.

"With Peyton?"Jamie asked

"Yes, and we have to do it right away because we don't have much time," Lily informed him.

Kyle lifted Lily from the ground and leaned her against a rock for support. He unclasped her bandeau and covered her peachy breasts with his lips. Lily put her hands around his shoulders and yielded with absolute abandon to the fiery lust that had almost consumed her. Kyle put his finger through the side of her short, so he could make a gap wide enough to fit in his hard meat. Lily cried out with passion as he penetrated her and her voice echoed through the still air. Kyle grunted as he rammed her like a wild bull. She screamed his name over and over again as he rode her to the ninth cloud.

Peyton eyed Jamie eagerly, and she could tell he was still bitter about what happened. She got and was about to walk away when Jamie held her by the arm as she walked past him. He quickly spun her around, bent her over, and tore off her thongs. Peyton wanted to protest but remembered Lily's warning and kept her cool. Jamie plunged his dick into her, and she screamed out loud. He pulled down the front of her sundress and squeezed her breasts so hard as he pounded her. Peyton screamed so hard she could be heard hundreds of miles away. Jamie pounded his anger on her cunt, and she squirmed like a kitten. His hot liquid shot a mile high into Peyton's pussy.

Lily went back into the orchard to get the diamond. She pulled it out from the stone, and it glowed brightly in her hands. It was clearer than a glass of water, and it looked so powerful. Lily put it into the locket she wore around her neck, and it fitted so perfectly.

"So where do we head to from here?" Jamie asked.

"To the Daffodil Manor," she smiled.

Peyton was so excited to be out of the place and hugged Jamie. Jamie pulled away gently, and the rejection hurt Peyton deeply.

"You're such a fool, Jamie, and I detest you so much," she exclaimed.

Lily and Kyle gasped in horror. Peyton had ruined their almost perfect exit.

Just like they feared, the ground started to shake, and Ibex began to crumble.

They scrambled over the cliff and hurried down the mountain just in time to find a cave a few meters from their ship. They ran into the cave and took shelter. The atmosphere suddenly felt so humid and sulphuric. They were all sweating profusely, and the air felt heavy, making it difficult for them to breathe. They watched in horror as the mountain spewed angry lava into the sky. Showers of molten magma shot into the sea as the ground trembled violently. The beautiful Ibex was rapidly crumbling into molten lava that flowed into the sea.

Lily figured out that they had to leave if they didn't want to sink with Ibex.

"We have to make a run for the ship if we are to leave here alive. There will be a lull for a few minutes, and that's when we move."

They heard a bird sing, and at Lily's instruction, they dashed the ship. The sea was hot enough to make a cup of coffee, and they barely made it into the vessel before the gangway melted away.

"Hey Kyle, we could do with more hands on the deck," Jamie called out to Kyle.

They quickly set sail just in time before a huge boulder was ripped by an unknown force and flung into the sea. The boat swayed dangerously, and they all screamed in fear.

EPILOGUE

"Rebecca, I'm sorry, okay."

Ron held a handpicked bouquet in front of Rebecca as a peace treaty. She smiled and tilted her face for his kiss. Ron's mouth devoured her lips hungrily, he had missed her taste, and he was starving for her touch. Rebecca broke the kiss and put the flowers aside before he reclaimed her lips. Rebecca melted in his arms, and she returned his kiss. She ran her hands all over his back, pulling him closer to her.

"Rebecca, I'm going to make love to you right here on this beach, Ron whispered.

They got on the sand, and Ron loosened her bikini straps, her breasts jumped free, and he covered her nipples with his mouth. Rebecca weaved her fingers through his hair as his tongue swirled around the nipple, making her burn with pure lust. She could feel his hard cock rubbing against her thighs. Rebecca spread her legs so she could feel his hard erection between her thighs. Her cunt craved for his special rhythm, his wild thrust, and the feel of his mouth against her most vulnerable spot.

The sound of Jer's voice as he approached the beach interrupted them. Ron gave a frustrated sigh and went off to swim in the sea while Rebecca talked to Jer. He had brought a bottle of wine and some glasses to celebrate the return of the voyagers.

"What do we do now, Bec," Jer asked Rebecca as they lay on the beach enjoying the sun. Ron had grown tired of being ignored and had gone for a swim.

"I don't know Jer, Cartoonia has chosen a new firestorm, and we have to depend on her if we want to get out of here," Rebecca replied.

"We?" Jer chuckled at the impossibility of everyone leaving Cartoonia.

"Jer, we are the uneven pair, remember? Cartoonia can only show the way to the even pair, so if we want to get Areeyah, we have to do as the girl says."

Jer gave her a sinister smile and stood up from his beach bed.

"Where are you going to?" Rebecca asked.

"I'm going for a swim."

Jer walked to the edge of the water and looked back at Rebecca. She waved at him, and he waved back. He brought out the four figurines that were hidden in his pocket. He scrutinized each one, and for the first time, he noticed the striking resemblance to the real-life versions of the figurines. Jer wondered if there was another way of disposing of the figurines.

"I wouldn't do that if I were you," a soft voice cooed behind him.

He turned around and saw Rebecca still sitting in her chair. He paused for a while and pretended to watch the waves. Jer raised his hands to throw away the figurines into the sea and felt someone grip his arm. He screamed and turned around to see Rebecca now standing behind him.

"What the hell are you doing, Jer?"

Jer was too shocked to say anything.

"Give them to me," Rebecca demanded.

Jer gave her a scathing look and threw the figurines into the sea.